# Fraid E. Cat

## By Al Newman
## Illustrated by Jim Doody

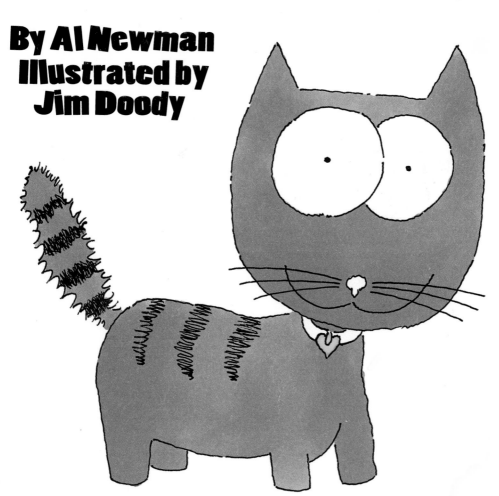

For a free color catalog describing Gareth Stevens' list of high-quality books, call 1-800-542-2595 (USA) or 1-800-461-9120 (Canada). Gareth Stevens' Fax: (414) 225-0377.

Library of Congress Cataloging-in-Publication Data available upon request from publisher. Fax: (414) 225-0377 for the attention of the Publishing Records Department.

ISBN 0-8368-1388-X

This edition first published in 1995 by
**Gareth Stevens Publishing**
1555 North RiverCenter Drive, Suite 201
Milwaukee, Wisconsin 53212, USA

First published in 1993 by Humanics Children's House, Humanics Limited, Atlanta, Georgia.
© 1993 Humanics Limited.

Printed in the United States of America

1 2 3 4 5 6 7 8 9 99 98 97 96 95

Gareth Stevens Publishing
**MILWAUKEE**

Fraid E. Cat is
very sweet—

just the kind of cat
you'd like to meet.

# She romps and runs

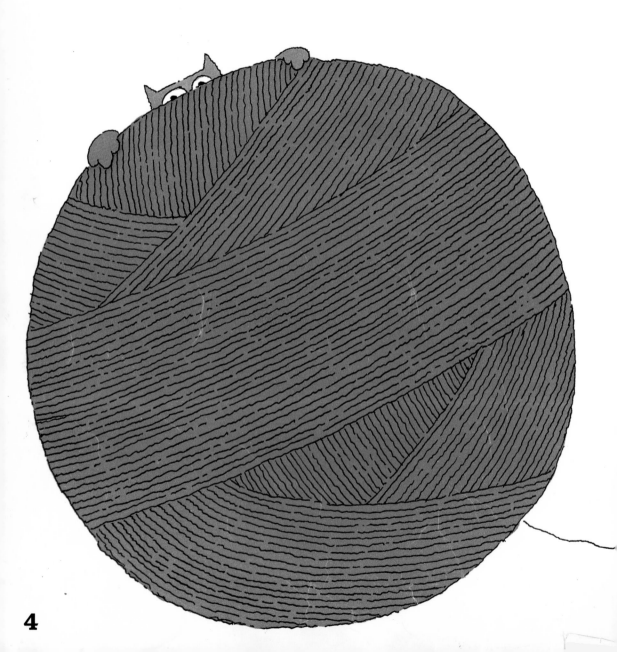

# and plays all day.

But when
it's time
to hit the hay,

# Fraid E. Cat
## won't say good night,

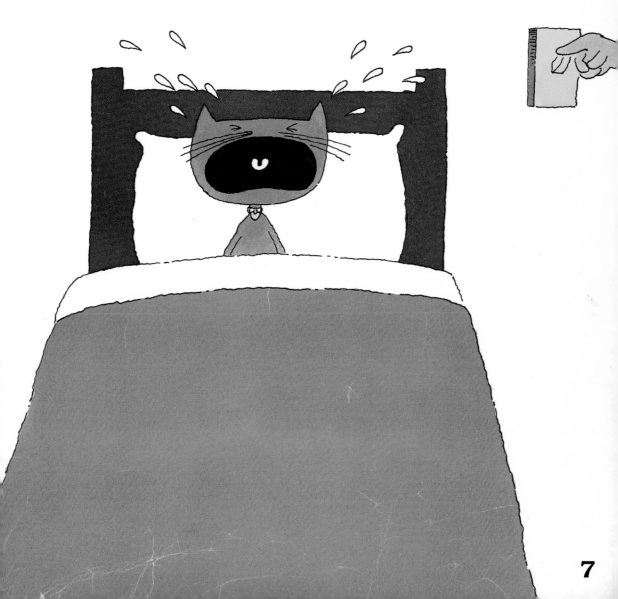

'cause she's afraid
to turn out the light.

Fraid E. Cat
is afraid of the dark!

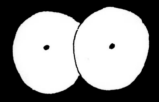

She imagines
things that just
aren't there.

Like a big old chair
that turns into a bear!

Or a little red wagon
that becomes a dragon!

Strange little noises
give her a fright.

She shivers and shakes
all through the night.

And when there's thunder
and lightning outside,

Fraid E. dives under
the covers to hide.

You've got to help
this cat.

Show her there's nothing
under the bed.

# Tell her the monsters

# are all in her head.

Let her look
in the closet

and behind the door.

# Then Fraid E. won't

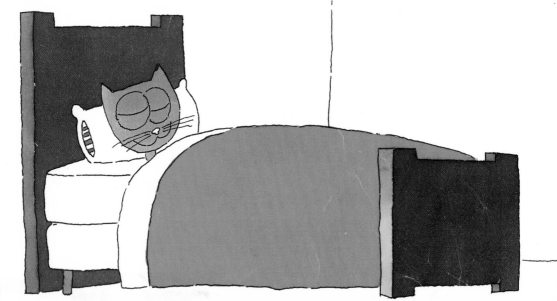

be afraid anymore.

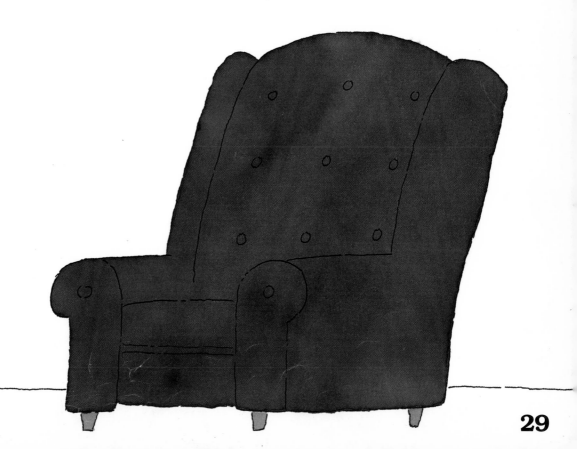

Now it's time to
say goodnight.

Let's close our eyes
and turn out the light.

# Good night!